With Thanks
& Appreciation

To _____

From _____

thank you, thanks, etc.: *I thank you* is now reserved for formal occasions or tongues; *thank you* is the ordinary phrase, but tends more and more to be lengthened with or without occasion into *thank you so much*, or *thank you very much*, often with the addition of *indeed* for good measure. *Thanks* is a shade less cordial than *thank you* and *many* and *best* and *a thousand thanks* and *thanks awfully* are frequent elaborations of it; *much thanks* is archaic, surviving through our familiarity with Francisco's *For this relief much thanks*, and now only used jocularly. The colloquial variant *Thanks a lot* is becoming popular. If an acknowledgement of thanks is felt to be needed it will be *Don't mention it*, or *Not at all* or, in U.S., *You're welcome*.

—*A Dictionary of Modern English Usage*
H. W. Fowler

With Thanks & Appreciation

The Sweet Nellie Book of
Thoughts, Sentiments,
Tokens & Traditions
of the Past

PAT ROSS

VIKING
STUDIO
BOOKS

VIKING STUDIO BOOKS
Published by the Penguin Group
Viking Penguin Inc., 40 West 23rd Street, New York, New York 10010, U.S.A.
Penguin Books Ltd, 27 Wrights Lane, London W8 5TZ, England
Penguin Books Australia Ltd, Ringwood, Victoria, Australia
Penguin Books Canada Ltd, 2801 John Street, Markham, Ontario, Canada L3R 1B4
Penguin Books (N.Z.) Ltd, 182-190 Wairau Road, Auckland 10, New Zealand

Penguin Books Ltd, Registered Offices: Harmondsworth, Middlesex, England

First published in 1989 by Viking Penguin Inc.
Published simultaneously in Canada

3 5 7 9 10 8 6 4 2

Copyright © Pat Ross, 1989   All rights reserved

LIBRARY OF CONGRESS CATALOGING IN PUBLICATION DATA
Ross, Pat.
With thanks & appreciation: the sweet Nellie book of thoughts,
sentiments, tokens & traditions of the past / Pat Ross.
p.   cm.
1. Etiquette–Quotations, maxims, etc.   2. Interpersonal
relations–Quotations, maxims, etc.   3. Thank-you notes.   I. Title.
II. Title: With thanks and appreciation.
PN6084.E85R67   1989
395'.4–dc19   88-17140
ISBN 0 670 82521 2

Printed In Singapore By Times Offset Pte. Ltd.

Set in Nicholas Cochin. Designed by Amy Hill.

AN APPRECIATION

Certainly a book of this title would not be complete without its own words of gratitude. And so I would like to thank the industrious Leisa Crane for her dedication and good ideas; Patti O'Shaughnessy for her usual and unusual creative input; my mother, Anita Kienzle, for eagerly dusting off our old books and finding wonderful treasures; my grandmother Jennie Walsh Hooper for sharing her early books on etiquette and entertainment; Sandy Washburn at The Cottage at Chappaqua and Bonnie Ferris of Bonnie Ferris Antiques for loaning me pieces from their shops and personal collections; A Touch of Ivy for the vintage wallpaper; and, of course, the supportive staff at Sweet Nellie.

I would also like to acknowledge the following for assistance in research: The New York Society Library, The Cooper-Hewitt

Museum (especially Margaret Luckars), The New York Public Library, The Museum of American Folk Art.

There is never enough love and thanks for my husband, Joel, and daughter, Erica, who have learned to "appreciate" take-out meals on a regular basis.

Last, but not least, it's good to be back on the side of the publisher, with special thanks to Michael Fragnito of Viking for his belief in new projects and Sweet Nellie; and to Barbara Williams and Amy Hill for their fine work on a tight schedule. We all thank Regina Hayes, the editor of my children's books at Viking, for putting us together; and Amy Berkower, my smart agent, for keeping us that way!

INTRODUCTION

I learned to write bread-and-butter notes when I was old enough to understand social obligation. My notes were filled with elaborate and profuse thanks, even if I did not particularly like the gift or the person who gave it. These notes became a sort of wonderful prose and poetry exercise for me, written on grown-up paper—heavy, smooth, and white—and I thoroughly enjoyed the custom.

The tradition of expressing thanks has made poets and artists of ordinary folk throughout the ages. The best example of this tradition is the nineteenth-century calling card—a tiny decorative canvas of sorts, often expressing pleasant sentiments in verse. Today these calling cards, with their fine calligraphy and colorful flourishes, are treasured folk art tokens. Their diminutive embellishments and timeless charm inspired this book in part and occupy the heart of it.

Although the etiquette of the nineteenth and early twentieth centuries is often thought of today as excessive and even humorous, with its attention to every detail, there has been a heartening return to good manners and gracious behavior. It is important to look back on occasion to see what may have been lost, and to retrieve those traditions.

Etiquette books of the day were filled with advice on letter and note writing: the correct color ink, the proper form, the appropriate stationery. Frequently a note or letter accompanied some small gift—intricate needlework, a true labor of love; a smartly bound book; a bouquet of pansies; a basket of freshly picked apples; a hand-knit shawl; a box of bonbons.

No longer is anyone expected to execute perfect penmanship or compose eloquent verse to express thanks. There's generally a greeting card, note card, or ready-made gift to fit every occasion. Yet most of us are constantly searching for creative ways to say thank you and to express appreciation for a weekend visit, an unforgettable meal, the perfect gift, or, simply, someone's thoughtfulness. At these times, one does well to recall the niceties of the past.

With Thanks & Appreciation remembers many traditions that we cherish today, and still carry on in changed but meaningful ways.

On the
Bread-and-Butter
Obligation...

he phrase "bread-and-butter note" (or letter) became the accepted term for a written form of thanks for entertainment or hospitality about 1900. Such hospitality was symbolized by the providing of bread and butter—the familiar term for everyday food.

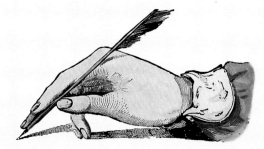

If you make a mistake in a word, draw your pen through it, or score it so as to be quite illegible, and then interline the correction, placing a caret beneath. This will be better than scratching out the error with your penknife, and afterward trying to write a new word in the identical place.

—*The Behaviour Book:*
A Manual for Ladies
Miss Leslie
1853

When you write to your friends, make your letters so beautiful in form and text that they will be read, re-read, and cherished a long time after as a fond memory. It will be a big step on the road to social perfection.

—*Book of Etiquette*
Lillian Eichler
1922

Francis W. Crowninshield, a turn-of-the-century etiquette expert, suggested in Manners for the Metropolis (1909) that it was de rigueur to compose a bread-and-butter letter or a "pleaser" after a weekend visit, offering the following "safe" opening sentence for such a letter:

How kind you were to open the gates of Heaven and give me that little glimpse of Paradise.

Avoid in writing, as in talking, all words that
do not express true meaning.

—*The Behaviour Book:
A Manual for Ladies*
Miss Leslie
1853

If I tell you I value it more highly than a letter, it is not solely on
account of its greater intrinsic value nor because I wanted what you
sent but because it is another proof of your consideration and regard.
To me it is acceptable because of the labor and trouble it has cost you
and the satisfaction I shall feel in wearing them—a voluntary offering
from my best friend bearing evidence of her handiwork and industry.

—From a letter received in 1855
in response to the gift of a pair
of hand-embroidered slippers, in
Decorative Arts of Victoria's Era
Frances Lichten
1950

The thoughts contained in a letter, the kind, unselfish, pretty thoughts of friendship, remain forever in the heart and mind of the person for whom it was intended.

—*Book of Etiquette*
Lillian Eichler
1922

Then there are young ladies born with the organ of letter-writing amazingly developed and increased by perpetual practice.

—*The Behaviour Book:
A Manual for Ladies*
Miss Leslie
1853

Don't make the children say things that they do not want to [in letters of thank you]. Protect them from the petty insincerities of social life as long as possible.

—*Book of Etiquette*
Lillian Eichler
1922

True hospitality neither expects nor desires any return, and it is only the inhospitable that keep a debt and credit account.

—*Sensible Etiquette*
of the Best Society
Mrs. W. O. Ward
1878

Wax seals that were used to securely fasten envelopes also enabled the sender to individualize a letter with tiny messages stamped into the wax.

Sealing wax fell into disfavor in the United States, however, when cross-country letters passing through the heat of the Isthmus of Panama became irretrievably glued together, blurring addresses and confusing the postmaster as well.

A thoughtful book on social etiquette published in 1908, *The Social Fetich* by *Lady Grove*, suggested that the ending of letters has a distinctly ascending scale of warmth. The author's scale was as follows:

yours truly

yours very truly

yours sincerely

yours very sincerely

yours most truly

yours most sincerely

yours ever

yours affectionately

yours very affectionately

yours most affectionately

your loving

your very loving

your most loving

In taking leave of the hostess, it is necessary to thank her cordially. Criticisms, either of the conduct of some other guest, or of servants, are poor form and should be avoided. The ideal guest is the one who has that ease and poise of manner, that calmness and kindness of temper, that loving and lovable disposition that makes people somehow want to talk to and be with him.

—*Book of Etiquette*
Lillian Eichler
1922

On the
Calling Card
Tradition...

The social calling card dates back to the *Stone Age*, when the head of one family would on occasion leave a roughly carved block of stone at the door of another. This was the ultimate expression of goodwill and friendship. As the tradition evolved, the block of stone was, fortunately, replaced by a small rectangular piece of paper. During the nineteenth century, this calling card was frequently embellished with hand-drawn decorations and verse. But by the beginning of the twentieth century, the baroquely decorated card had been replaced by a plainer, more formal name card.

The leaving of cards was, among other things, an important way of saying thanks, especially to a hostess for a meal or a visit in the country. They were often left in a tray in the hallway when the caller took tea.

One of the most popular keepsakes of the day was the Ladies'
Album, a book of handwritten verses, testimonials, drawings, and calling
cards contributed by the owner's friends and visitors.

One fair owner stated on the first leaf of her book:

> This little book, with all the prose
> Its varied page imparts,
> I dedicate to gentle eyes
> And sympathising hearts.
> Then all who bring their smile or tear
> May tearless drop the gem
> For commonsense shall ne're come here
> To praise them or condemn.

Autograph albums became cherished possessions. Greetings to be written were often taken from autograph-verse books published specifically for that purpose.

Fond memory, come and hover o'er
This album page of my fair friend;
Enrich her from thy precious store,
And happy recollections send.
If on this page she chance to gaze
In years to come—where'er she be—
Tell her of earlier happy days,
And bring her back one thought of me.

The printing of ready-made decorative calling and name cards became big business. A card in black and white could be hand-colored by the sender and then signed, adding a personal touch.

The friendliest sentiments are expressed by a timely card . . . It tells its little story of fondness or of indifference, according to the promptness and the method of its arrival. It announces a friend, and it says adieu. It congratulates delicately, but unmistakably, and it is the brief bearer of tidings which a volume could explain with no more clearness.

—*Social Etiquette of New York*
1879

Would that this garland fair
Might weave around thy life,
A spell to shield from care,
A guard from every strife.

—Verse from a nineteenth-century
calling card, to be enclosed
with a gift of flowers

olding down a corner of one's calling card held great significance. If the bottom right-hand corner was turned down, it meant a personal call; the top right-hand corner meant condolence; the bottom left-hand corner meant congratulations.

When we are old we'll smile and say
We had no cares in childhood's day
But we'll be wrong. 'Twill not be true.
I've this much care. I care for you.

—Verse from a nineteenth-century
calling card

Ever to think of thee

My card and my compliments.
Please give yours in exchange.

—Preprinted card

After 1870, beautiful chirography (pen decoration) was left to the professional penman, an itinerant who—for a very small sum—elaborately scrolled the customer's name on a package of calling cards, adorning them with flourishes of birds, ribbons, swans, quill pens, and eagles.

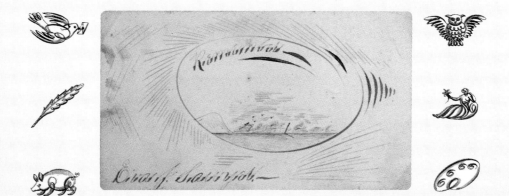

Though small the gift to thee I send
Acceptance let it meet
For even trifles from a friend
In friendship's eyes are sweet.

—Hand-scripted verse from
Philena Kendall's 1843
friendship album,
Philadelphia

Forget not ah! forget not me,
When evening shades descend
For thou my thoughts still ...
My fondly cherished friend.

Remember

*On
Gift Appreciation...*

The tradition of giving flowers is cherished and age-old. It replaces words of thanks with posies selected for their symbolic meaning.

Periwinkle: Pleasures of memory
Bell Flower: Gratitude
Agrimony: Thoughtfulness
Bay Wreath: Reward of merit
Garden Sage: Esteem
Campanula: Gratitude

This mid-nineteenth-century poem commemorates the offering of a gift basket from a Shaker woman to the ministry.

BASKET OF APPLES

Come, come my beloved
And sympathize with me
Receive the little basket
And the blessing so free

In the Victorian era, the desire to publicly proclaim virtuous sentiments was carried into the realm of intricate needlework, samplers, cross-stitch, and woolwork.

Perforated paper cards punched with minute holes became a substitute for canvas in a proliferation of needlework bookmarks, a popular and universally accepted gift.

Nineteenth- and early-twentieth-century "album quilts" were conclusive proof that one was held in high regard by one's friends. Contributors to the quilt would embroider or write their names in ink on quilt blocks that would later be pieced and quilted by the designated quilters and then presented as a gift. Quilts of this kind were often decorated with floral and geometric piecework and appliqué techniques appropriate to the occasion. The scrapbook-like quality of this type of quilt endeared it to its owner.

"Dame Curtsey's" Book of Novel Entertainment for Every Day in the Year (*Ellyn Howell Glover, 1907*) *suggested appropriate poems to enclose with various gifts.*

With a pair of gloves as a Valentine:

A little hand, a soft white hand,
A hand I know't is thine
These gloves will fit. So may I ask
That gloves and hand be mine?

With an umbrella:

Open me and raise me high;
And in damp weather keep me nigh;
Or, even when the sun shines bright,
I'll keep its rays from you all right.

With a mirror:

In this glass may you see smiles.

With a humorous book:

> A little nonsense now and then
> Is relished by the wisest men.

With a cup and saucer:

> When out of this cup you are drinking your tea,
> Perchance you will think kindly of me.

With a work basket:

> Industry can do any thing which
> genius can do, and very many things
> which it cannot.

With a purse:

> May your purse be heavy
> and your heart light.

With a wedding gift:

> God saw thee most fit for me.

With a bottle of wine:

One sip of this will bathe the drooping spirits in delight.

With a musical program:

If you love music, hear it.

With a book:

This little paper traveller goes forth to your door, charged with tender greetings. Pray you, take him in. He comes from a house where you are well-beloved.

With a heart-shaped locket:

My heart is as true as steel.

With a knitted shawl:

This little shawl was knit for you, By one who loves you fond and true.

With a piece of one's own work:

Alone I did it.

With a volume of poems:

Wise poets that wrap truth in tales.

With a watercolor:

A pleasure that can never pall,
A serene moment deftly caught and kept
To make immortal summer on your wall.

With a box of candy:

Sweets to the sweet.

With a pen wiper:

Perchance thou'lt write a line to me.
Your letter being finished, then
Here's wherewithal to wipe your pen.

Mothering Sunday, celebrated on the fourth Sunday in Lent, was an English tradition, a precursor of what we now know as Mother's Day, and honored the father as well. A special dinner of the mother's favorite foods was prepared by children and grandparents. The table was set with place cards bearing suitable quotations:

God cannot be everywhere,
so He made mothers.

—Arab proverb

and

A mother is a mother still,
the holiest thing alive.

—Samuel Taylor Coleridge

On the subject of gifts and appreciation on Mothering Sunday, "Dame Curtsey's" Book of Novel Entertainment advises: "If it is not possible for children to be present, they can send a letter of love and devotion, with a gift either large or small, which will be cherished by the dear household saints, brightening the sunset path for the ofttimes weary feet."

Unlike this fragile flowers
That blooms and fades away
My love for thee hath power
To bloom and bloom for aye !

The problem of entertaining a turn-of-the-century child embarking on a long journey was solved in "Dame Curtsey's" Book of Novel Entertainment *with this clever gift idea.*

A friend provided a huge ball of worsted, with instructions to unwind one "surprise" a day. The ball contained all kinds of little novelties: a top, dolls of various sizes, a wee bottle of perfumery, a handkerchief, a pair of round-pointed scissors, small boxes of odd shapes filled with hard bonbons, toy animals from a Noah's Ark, a coarse needle, and a box of kindergarten beads.

On
Grateful Hearts...

Gratitude is a very pleasant sensation, both for those who feel and to those who excite it. No one who confers a favor can say *with truth* that they "want no thanks." They always do.

—*The Behaviour Book: A Manual for Ladies*
Miss Leslie
1853

There is no pleasure in empty ceremony, formal parade, and idle display! How often would this cry be echoed from the hearts of the merely fashionable, if they would but declare their real sentiments!

—*Keeping House and House Keeping*
Mrs. Sarah J. Hale
1845

Gratitude is the memory of the heart.

—Jean-Baptiste Massieu
in a letter to the
Abbé Sicard, c. 1800

Sweet is the breath of vernal shower,
The bee's collected treasures sweet,
Sweet music's melting fall, but sweeter yet
The still small voice of Gratitude.

—Thomas Gray
"Ode for Music"
1769

Gratitude is a fruit of great cultivation; you do
not find it among gross people.

—Samuel Johnson in
*The Journal of a Tour to the Hebrides
with Samuel Johnson, LL.D.*
by James Boswell, 1785

Swift gratitude is sweetest; if it delays, all gratitude is empty—unworthy of the name.

—Anonymous

In every thing give thanks . . .

—1 Thessalonians 5:18

What takes our heart must merit our esteem.

—Matthew Prior
Solomon on the Vanity of the World
1718

Sweet as love, or the remembrance of a generous deed.

—*The Prelude*, Book VI
William Wordsworth
1850

You have particular reason to place confidence
in those who have shown affection for you in
your early days, when you were incapable of
making them any return.

—*Principles of Politeness
and of Knowing the World*
Lord Chesterfield
1886

Unclassified
Laws of Etiquette

Never present a gift saying that it is of no use to yourself.

Never accept of favors and hospitalities without rendering an exchange of civilities when opportunity offers.

—*Hill's Manual*
Thomas E. Hill
1885

Life is short, but there is always time for courtesy.

—Ralph Waldo Emerson
Uncollected Lectures
1932

*On
Rewards of Merit
Well Deserved...*

ewards of Merit were formal certificates presented to children in the nineteenth century as praise for some job well done, whether academic or social. These small documents were often preprinted, with blank spaces for the name of the child and the instructor or parent. The Rewards of Merit most valuable today, however, were drawn entirely by hand and thoughtfully inscribed especially for an individual child.

EXCELSIOR!

THIS IS A CERTIFICATE OF

FIFTY MERITS,

PRESENTED T

Mabel S. Pierc

for Good Conduct from _____

to _____

Susie S. Lu

Oct 27 18 *8*

REWARD OF MERIT

PRESENTED TO _____

By _____ TEACHER

t seems fitting that a book about traditions of the past should be decorated with period artwork. In that spirit, the art in With Thanks & Appreciation has been taken from personal collections of original nineteenth-century calling cards and other paper treasures of the time.

The endpapers and chapter openings contain patterns reproduced from some of our favorite original vintage wallpapers.